Scary Spider
and the Underpants

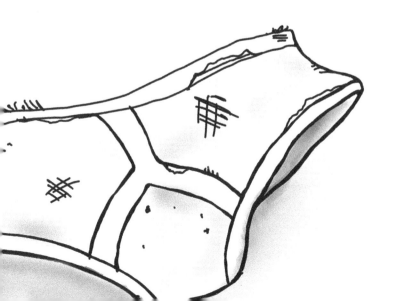

Studio 22 Publishing

Words by: Dave West
Pictures by: Steve Pearse
© 2021

The right of Dave West to be identified as the author and Steve Pearse as
the illustrator of this Work has been asserted by them in accordance with the
Copyright, Designs and Patents Act 1988. All rights reserved.

This book is sold subject to the condition that it shall not, by way of trade
or otherwise, be lent, resold, hired out or otherwise circulated without the
publisher's prior consent, in any form of binding or cover other than that
in which it is published, and without a similar condition, including this
condition, being imposed on the subsequent purchaser.

Typeset in Parma Petit.

Published in Great Britain in 2021.

Scary Spider
and the Underpants
the

For Mia

It was a
beautiful day
but Spider

was in a

bad mood.

He **was** hungry.

He used to **catch** so many flies, he would **give** some away.

But, today he'd **forgotten**
how to **spin a web**.
And he was really
hungry.

So he tried **catching** flies
with a fishing rod...

...with a net...

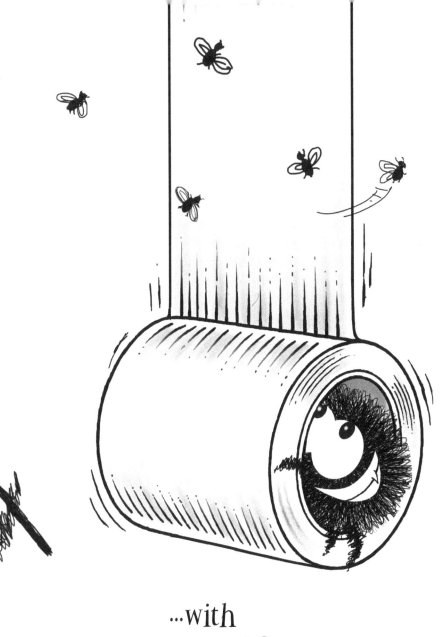

...with
sticky tape.

He even **tried** knitting a **web.**

But nothing worked.
Now he was
starving.

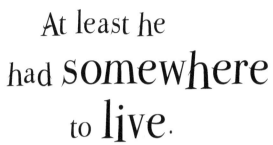

At least he
had somewhere
to live.

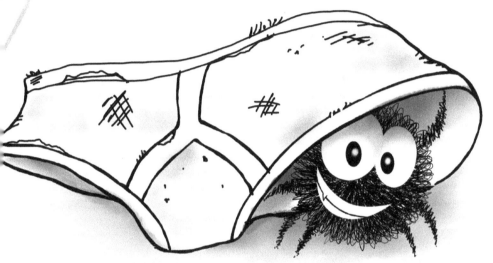

This old pair of
underpants made
the perfect home.

They were nice
and **warm** but
they had a really
funny **smell**.

It reminded him of...

Popcorn?

No. Not that.

Smelly old
socks?

Not that
either.

Yellow
crayons?

Hmm. Maybe.

Just then,
he let out an
almighty

It was so
loud, the
room **shook**,
and everything
went **dark**.

The next thing **Spider** knew, he was sitting in the **middle** of the most **beautiful** web he'd **ever** seen.

21

He wasn't **hungry** anymore.

He had so many flies he *gave* some away.

The End.

Did you know?

The world's oldest spider lived to the grand old age of 43.

Spiders have blue blood.

Fear of spiders is called 'Arachnophobia'.

Spider silk is stronger than steel.

When the web is finished with, the spider eats it.

Spiders do go fishing.

Lightning Source UK Ltd.
Milton Keynes UK
UKHW051430171221
395713UK00008B/334